The Big Show

DON TREMBATH

THE BLACK BELT SERIES

ORCA BOOK PUBLISHERS

National Library of Canada Cataloguing in Publication Data
Trembath, Don, 1963-

  The big show / Don Trembath.

ISBN 1-55143-266-8

I. Title. II. Series: Trembath, Don, 1963- Black belt series.

PS8589.R392B53 2003   jC813'.54   C2003-910063-4

PZ7.T71925Bi 2003

First published in the United States: 2003

Library of Congress Control Number: 2003100412

Summary: Charlie, Sidney and Jeffrey take part in a karate
tournament. All must face personal issues before stepping into the
ring.

Orca Book Publishers gratefully acknowledges the support for its
publishing programs provided by the following agencies: the
Government of Canada through the Book Publishing Industry
Development Program (BPIDP), the Canada Council for the Arts,
and the British Columbia Arts Council.

Cover design: Christine Toller
Cover illustration: Dean Griffiths
Printed and bound in Canada

05 04 03 • 5 4 3 2 1

IN CANADA:
Orca Book Publishers
1030 North Park Street
Victoria, BC Canada
V8T 1C6

IN THE UNITED STATES:
Orca Book Publishers
PO Box 468
Custer, WA   USA
98240-0468

To my friends who do the real Beeeg Show,
a performance group like no other.
See you in the summer.

DT

1.

Tizzy Martin dropped four teaspoons of sugar into her cup, then poured herself some tea and lit a cigarette.

It was her day off, so she was not made up. Her usually striking face was dimmed by dark circles under her eyes, and her forehead was creased with lines from frowning and worry. Her hair — long and brown and magnificently curly when washed — flopped on her head like a large, empty nest that had fallen hard from a tall tree.

Tizzy was under a lot of stress. Work at the restaurant was going well. The worthless pill of a new assistant manager who had been trying for weeks to coax her out on a date had finally accepted the fact that "not on your life" meant "no," so it was not any of the usual things that was causing her grief. Yet it was not something entirely new either. It was her son, Sidney, who was sitting across from her at the table, sipping a cup of tea of his own and looking as defiant as ever.

Tizzy recognized the look. It was like she was staring into a mirror.

"So, you don't know what I'm talking about," she said, pulling hard on her smoke. She was a single mom, and a proud one at that, but at times like this one, a little help would have been appreciated.

"Nope," said Sidney, a small, fiery boy with a brush cut, lean muscles and a lightning quick temper.

"Not a clue?"

"Not a clue."

Tizzy took a sip of her tea. "Let me try this then. In two weeks you become a teenager."

Sidney smiled. "I know."

"You take a gigantic step towards becoming a man."

"You got that right."

"And you say good-bye to being a little boy."

Sidney wavered. "Not really."

"Yes, you do."

"I'll only be thirteen."

"You'll never be called a boy again. You'll be called a teen."

"So?"

"People will start treating you differently."

"It's about time."

"They'll start treating you more like an adult than a child."

"That's all right."

"And all those years you've had to prepare yourself for this moment will be gone."

Sidney frowned. This was the same point where she had lost him the first time around. "Who says the first twelve years of my life were for preparation? I was having fun."

"Exactly," said Tizzy, blowing smoke into the air.

"What's wrong with that?"

"You're about to find out."

"Find out what?"

"What's so wrong with it."

"Wrong with what?"

"Goofing around. Fighting with anyone who looks at you the wrong way. Getting in trouble with your teachers."

Sidney sat back in his chair and stared at his mother. Whatever she was talking about was so far beyond him he couldn't reach it with a ladder. "Are you saying that I've wasted my life so far?"

Tizzy butted her cigarette in the ashtray. "Not exactly."

"Are you saying that I haven't done as much with my life as I could have?"

"That's more like it."

"Well, look at you," he said. He was not afraid to talk to his mother this way. They were a combative pair living together in a small, two-bedroom apartment in a small Alberta town where no two people stayed strangers for very long.

"Look at me what?"

"You're turning thirty-two on the same day I'm turning thirteen. What have you done with your life that's so amazing?"

"I had you."

"What else?"

"I've raised you on my own."

"Not very well, apparently."

Tizzy reached for another cigarette. She knew she was flawed as a mother. She knew much of Sidney's ferocious temper came from her, and that the number of tantrums she had thrown in front of him had done little to teach him self-control.

"I've done the best I could, given the situation."

"That you created," Sidney finished.

Tizzy sat on that comment for a moment. She had thrown Sidney's father out of their lives for numerous reasons and had failed miserably at finding a replacement. She had never gone on welfare, choosing instead to work the long, shifting hours of a waitress at a popular restaurant and bar on the edge of town. She read to her son every night she was home until she could no longer keep her eyes open, and then he would read to her.

"We all make mistakes," she said. "It's what you do with them that makes the difference."

"Is that Oprah talking?" said Sidney.

"No. It's me. And it's true. And you should listen because your days of being a kid are over."

"They're not over."

"They're about to be."

"I'm still a kid."

"You're a teenager."

"What's the difference?"

"You're about to find out."

"No, I'm not."

"That's what I said. Now I'm thirty-two."

Sidney sat and again stared at his mother.

He was not the deepest kid who ever walked down the street, and the time he spent thinking long and hard about his future could be counted with the second hand on the clock, but there was something about the message his mom was sending that was getting to him.

He stood and carried his teacup to the kitchen sink. "I've got karate after school," he said, ending the conversation. "I won't be home till around 6:00."

"Say hi to the boys," said Tizzy, meaning Sidney's friends, Charlie and Jeffrey.

"I'll invite them to my birthday party."

"Are you having one?" said Tizzy, who wasn't sure.

"Not anymore," said Sidney.

He let the door slam shut on his way out.

2.

Sidney did not go looking for Charlie after school, but he found him anyway, in the cafeteria, eating a hamburger.

With nothing better to do, he walked over and sat down beside him.

They were not the best of friends, these two. They knew each other from school, and over the past few months they had slowly become pals through the karate classes they took together.

"Hey," said Sidney, without much enthusiasm. He was still bothered by the conversation he had had with his mom.

"Hey," said Charlie back, pulling a copy of *Vanity Fair* magazine from his backpack.

Charlie was a hefty kid with a mouth that never stopped and a knack for getting into and out of trouble. He lived at home with his mom and dad and four older sisters.

Charlie quickly scanned each page until he found what he was looking for.

"Look at this," he said to Sidney, turning the magazine around. "Look at this girl." He was showing Sidney a full-page, glossy ad for blue jeans. "Is she hot or is she hot?"

Sidney, his mind elsewhere, glanced briefly at the ad. He shrugged.

Charlie turned the magazine back around so he could see the picture. "She is hot," he said, nodding his head as if to agree with himself. "She is sizzling hot."

The girl he was looking at had long, kinky black hair and thick pouty lips. Her eyes were wide and innocent and staring at him with such intensity and beauty that he wanted to reach out and touch her, or at least find out what her name was. "If she walked in here right now," he said, with absolute conviction and without taking his eyes off her, "I would walk right up to her and tell her that I will never eat another hamburger again, for as long as I'm alive."

Sidney ignored everything Charlie was saying and glanced around the cafeteria. He thought about buying himself a snack. He had thirty minutes to kill before karate started.

"I would say to her, you are the most beautiful thing in this world. You make my heart beat. You make my blood flow. You make my pulse do whatever a pulse does."

Sidney counted the small amount of change he had left over from lunch.

"I would put that in a poem and hand it to her," said Charlie.

Sidney put the change back in his pocket and shook his head. He was in a heavy mood and was not up for Charlie and his antics. "Look at you, Charlie," he said.

"Look at me what?" said Charlie, finally raising his eyes from the picture.

"My mom's giving me the business about wasting my life and you're sitting here falling in love with a picture in a stupid magazine."

Charlie frowned. "This is a real girl, Sidney. It's not just a picture."

"I know. And you're a real guy eating a real hamburger for about the millionth time in your life, and no one on this earth is going to stop you from eating a million and one. Or a million and two. Or a million and three."

Charlie went back to his girlfriend. "She could."

"No, she couldn't."

"If she walked in here right now . . . "

Charlie did not have a chance to finish his sentence. Sidney grabbed the magazine from him and shoved it to the end of the table.

"Did you even hear what I said?" said Sidney, his face red.

Charlie hesitated as he realized that his friend was experiencing some kind of personal crisis.

"Just now? Like two seconds ago? Did you hear what I said?"

Charlie had to think. To be honest, he had not been listening very closely to what Sidney was saying. He had been too engrossed in the picture of the girl.

"I said my mom is giving me the business about me wasting my life. She thinks I've gotten into too many fights and caused too much trouble. She thinks I'm nothing."

Charlie zeroed in. He could actually remember hearing that once before.

"I'm turning thirteen in two weeks and she's telling me that my days for preparing myself for adulthood are over."

Charlie tried to come up with something to say.

"Like I was supposed to just know that the

first twelve years of life are nothing more than a training ground for the next eighty?"

Charlie saw his chance. "You think you're gonna live 'til you're ninety-two?" he said, breaking his silence.

Sidney rolled his eyes. "Ninety-two. Fifty-two. Twenty-two. What's the difference? I've wasted the first twelve years of my life. That's what I'm talking about. I can't have any of them back. That doesn't make me feel very good."

"Why would you want them back?" said Charlie.

"To do them over again. Get them right."

"I wouldn't want to do them over again."

Sidney sat back in his chair and crossed his arms. "Sure you would, if you had the chance."

"No, I wouldn't."

"Maybe you wouldn't be so fat next time. Or have such a big mouth. Maybe you'd be allergic to hamburgers and you couldn't eat them even if you wanted to."

Charlie started to nod. "Maybe," he said. "Or maybe I'd do the exact same thing all over again, and I'd be twice the person I am now."

"Maybe you would," said Sidney, giving in.

"On the other hand," said Charlie, looking reflective, "maybe I'd be tall and dark and ripped, and I'd have girls like her knocking on my door every night." He motioned towards the magazine.

"Maybe that too," said Sidney.

"That wouldn't be so bad."

"Why not give yourself a mustache and an Italian accent to go with it?" said Sidney.

Charlie thought for a moment. "I could live with that."

"You could walk around like Casanova."

"Like who?"

"Casanova. Some guy who loved women all the time."

"I could live with that, too," said Charlie, nodding his head.

Sidney rolled his eyes again and released a frustrated sigh.

Charlie sat back and glanced towards the doors of the cafeteria. He saw a figure that made his eyes widen with horror, and his fantasy lurched to a stop. His jaw dropped open. All thoughts of love dashed from his head like evacuees from a house fire.

His sister Crystal was standing in the hallway. She was looking for something, or someone. She had a bag in her hand, and when she saw Charlie, she gave a look of complete annoyance and walked towards him.

Charlie stared at her in shock. Crystal did not go to his school. She was fifteen and she went to the high school. She had not publicly acknowledged Charlie's existence in her life since he had started walking on his own eleven years ago.

Crystal was shorter than Charlie and much, much slimmer. She had long, wavy brown hair and new wire-framed glasses that accentuated — in her opinion — her stunning brown eyes and — also in her own opinion — her big ugly nose. She was the youngest of his four sisters.

"Here, Einstein," she said, tossing him the bag when she was close to the table. "It's your pajamas."

"My what?" said Charlie, still stunned.

"Your pajamas. Or whatever you call that stupid outfit you wear in karate."

"My *gi*?" said Charlie.

"Whatever."

"I forgot it at home?"

"No. I took it out of your locker and ran home and washed it so it would be extra clean for your class tonight. Yes, you forgot it. And if it happens again, you can go to class in your underwear for all I care because I am not coming back here. I don't care what Mom says.

Now pay up." She held out her hand, palm up. "Two dollars. Let's go. I don't have all day."

Charlie sat motionless and stared at his sister.

"Come on, Kung-fu. I'm on my way to the store."

"I don't have two dollars," he said, snapping back to attention. In truth, he had four dollars in his front pocket, but a small Crispy Crunch Blizzard from Dairy Queen was three-something, and he had been looking forward to one all day.

"You do so."

"No, I don't."

"You do so."

"I do not."

"Don't lie to me, Charlie."

"I'm not."

"Then give me the bag back."

"What?"

"Give me the bag back."

"Forget it."

"You forget it. You don't have my money, so give me back the bag."

"Get your own."

"What do you mean, 'Get my own'? It's a stupid bag with a pair of pajamas in it. Now give it back until you get me my money."

"I told you. It's called a *gi*," said Charlie.

"I don't care what it's called. I did you a favor by bringing it down here. The least you can do is pay me for it. And I'm not getting out of your face until you do. Borrow some money from your friend here, or dig a little deeper into your pockets to find some."

Charlie struggled for a way out. He knew she wasn't leaving until she got what she was asking for. Unless, of course, he could convince her that it was time to go.

"What store are you going to?" he said.

"None of your business."

"Are your bowels acting up again?"

Crystal's face turned to stone. Her eyes became lasers and the beams hit Charlie square in the center of his forehead.

"You looked a little backed up at breakfast this morning. I was going to ask, but — ."

Crystal started to steam. "Shut your mouth, little brother," she hissed quietly.

"Are you going to get some more of that stuff? That fast-acting gunk that cleans your tubes out all the time?" Charlie turned to Sidney. "My sister's been backed up a lot lately. It's got to do with her eating habits. She likes to stay slim, so she doesn't eat."

Crystal started to smolder.

"I tell her, 'Think health before beauty,' but does she listen? No way."

Crystal's nostrils flared.

"Mom gives her celery and carrots in her lunch, but she doesn't eat them. Then she gets stomach cramps because all that stuff is just sitting there inside her body, wanting to get out, but she won't let it."

"Charlie," said Crystal as a warning.

"Elimination problems, they call it," said Charlie, shaking his head. "It's not pretty. It's not pretty at all. I feel for her. I really do. I go twice a day and I feel terrific."

"You are dead, Charlie," said Crystal, her eyes burning.

Charlie turned back to his sister. "You should go home and have some hot bran water. That's what worked the last time."

"You are dead," said Crystal, again.

"But please, this time remember to turn the fan on when things start to move," said Charlie as she began to leave. "Man," he added, turning to Sidney. "The switch is right there beside the light, but she never turns it on."

Crystal stopped moving and gave Charlie one final, deadly stare. "You better hope you learn something tonight," she said, her finger as pointed and lethal as a knife, "because you and I are going to deal with this."

"I learn something every night in karate," said Charlie, stating the truth.

"Is that right?" said Crystal.

"You bet. Every class. Something new comes along."

"Well that's real good, Charlie. But you know what? You're still a joke. Mom thinks so. Dad. We all think so. This karate thing you're into? It's a big joke, and you're the punchline. So be ready, because I am not going to forget this. And if you think I'm worried that you've learned some kind of kick that might stop me from tearing your head off, you're wrong. You are absolutely, totally dead wrong."

With those words hanging in the air, Crystal left the cafeteria. Charlie gulped. He wondered if he had gone too far to save himself two bucks. Sidney, who had sat in silence during the entire exchange, thought that although the first twelve years of his life may not have been perfect, he had never experienced an encounter quite like the one he had just seen, and for that, he was most grateful.

3.   It was not news to Charlie that the rest of his family considered his involvement in karate somewhat odd and ridiculous.

For the most part, he couldn't blame them.

Even by the loosest definition, Charlie could not be considered athletic, and exercise was a foreign concept to him. His bicycle in the garage had thick cobwebs hanging between the spokes. His two-year-old running shoes gleamed as brightly today as they had on the shelf of The Running Center, where his mother had bought them for half-price during the big close-out sale. The baseball bat his uncle had bought for him on his ninth birthday had still never made contact with a ball.

Even the way Charlie joined karate had a

direct link with his relaxed attitude. After Charlie refused to take part in a cross-country run at school (he had chosen instead to walk to the store for some snacks), his phys ed teacher had sent him to the principal. Mr. Duncan, or Frog Face as he was known, had ordered him, with the intention of instilling a sense of purpose and direction into his life, to attend karate lessons. Now, after several months in the class, Charlie stood with ten other students in the school gymnasium (called a *dojo* during karate hours), his *gi* on and his new blue belt tightened securely around his waist, waiting for the class to begin.

It did not bother Charlie that no one took him seriously, or so he told himself. He didn't take them seriously either, so what difference did it make? So what if no one in his family knew that he had successfully completed the first two stages of karate, taking him all the way from a lowly white belt to a yellow belt and then up to a blue? Who cares? They'd just laugh anyway, wouldn't they? And write it all off as something that must be easy if Charlie could do it?

Sure they would.

He bent at the waist and slowly started to

loosen up. Beside him, Sidney was working over the heavy bag, thudding it with kick after kick, all of them well-executed roundhouse kicks that struck the bag at a point well above Charlie's head.

"That's a good-looking kick there, Sidney," he said, striking up a conversation, which was something he did whenever his nerves got the better of him. Talking and joking around was a release for Charlie, just as eating was. "I may have to borrow it when I go home tonight. Crystal's gonna be waiting for me with a broom-stick in her hand. Or a table lamp."

Sidney, still with some anxiety of his own to work through, kicked on without saying a word. Charlie reluctantly hit the floor for some groin stretches. He was pitifully inflexible. "You get out of it what you put into it," the boys' karate instructor, Sensei Willie Duncan, always said. Charlie knew firsthand that the comment was true. "Every day you try to do a little bit more, and then one day you'll turn around and see how far you've come."

Charlie bent his head and grunted as he tried to take his body to a new level of elastic-ity. He started to count to ten, but was inter-rupted.

"Come on, Charlie," said a voice behind him. "Don't just sit there. Stretch."

It was Jeffrey, the third member of the trio, walking in to join the class.

"I am stretching," said Charlie, stopping immediately and sitting up straight.

"No, you're not. My grandma can bend better than that, and she just had heart surgery."

Jeffrey Stewart was a slim, well-mannered boy who lived with his mother and his elderly grandparents. He was meek by nature and turned shockingly pink when confronted with anger or aggression.

Charlie and Sidney were the first and only friends Jeffrey had ever had. Over the past several months since their relationship began, he has been equal parts thankful for, and enormously distressed by, their companionship.

"She didn't just have surgery," said Charlie, clarifying a point and happy again to have someone to talk to. "She got out of the hospital over a month ago."

"She's eighty-five years old, Charlie," said Jeffrey.

"So?"

"So that's pretty old to be bending over."

"That's not the point."

"Sure it is."

"No, it's not."

"It's part of it."

"No. You said she just had surgery and she can still bend better than I can. I'm saying, she's been out of surgery for over a month now, and at her size, she can touch her toes without bending over anyway. So it's not even a fair comparison."

Jeffrey sat down and did the splits. "I'm not comparing."

"It's like holding up an apple and a banana and saying, 'Look how much longer this one is. I bet it tastes better than that short little round thing.'"

"What?" said Jeffrey, his face turning red with exertion.

"Or picking up a hammer and a wrench and saying, 'Now which one would I rather pound a nail with?'"

Jeffrey buried his head and shifted his position on the floor. "I have no idea what you're talking about, Charlie."

"I don't know what you're talking about either."

"All I know is, if you tried a little harder, you'd be a lot more flexible in a hurry."

"And all I know is, your grandma weighs fourteen pounds, and she walks all bent over anyway."

Jeffrey shook his head. "She's an old lady, Charlie. Her bones are getting softer by the day. She can barely carry herself anymore."

"Tell me that doesn't help her. No bones in the way. No muscles."

Jeffrey decided to give up. "Forget it, Charlie. Go back to doing what you were doing."

"I was stretching, and I'm trying to go back to it, but you keep talking."

"Whatever."

"No. Not whatever. I was stretching. I was doing what you're doing, but my body is different than yours."

"I realize that."

"I can't do the splits like that."

"You could try."

"My body is bigger and thicker than yours. There's more stuff to move around."

"You can say that again."

"So, I'm doing the best I can here."

"If you say so."

"And with what I have to work with, I think I'm doing pretty well."

"Good for you."

"So it would be nice if you and Sidney and my sisters and Mom and Dad would just back off and leave me alone once in awhile."

Jeffrey stopped stretching and took a look at Charlie.

"You know? They think I'm a joke. You think I'm a joke."

"I never said you were a joke," said Jeffrey, taking note of the sudden change in tone of the conversation.

"They think I can't ever do anything right because I don't take anything seriously."

"I've never said that," said Jeffrey.

"Well, you've thought it, and so have they. So has everybody."

Charlie stopped talking and took a deep breath.

"I've never said that," said Jeffrey again.

"You just did. You said I could be more flexible if I just tried harder. That's the same as saying if I took it more seriously."

"Well, that's true, though," said Jeffrey, sticking with the honest approach. "You would be more flexible if you tried harder."

"That's what I'm talking about. Maybe I just don't want to be."

"Okay," said Jeffrey. "Fine."

"And when I do want to do it, I'll do it. On my own. Without telling anyone. And you guys will all see."

"Good for you."

"Then we'll see who's calling who a joke."

Jeffrey started to stretch again. Then he stopped. "I've never called you a joke, Charlie. And I've never thought it either."

"Well, they do," said Charlie, calming down a little. "All the time. And it's starting to bug me."

With that, Charlie wiggled his legs a wee bit farther apart and tried once again to stretch himself to new limits.

Jeffrey remained still and watched Charlie at work, then he flipped himself over to his back and started doing crunches to harden his stomach.

For a moment, it looked like they were both doing their very best.

4. For Sidney and Charlie, the situation was more or less the same: they were each looking for a chance to prove themselves.

Sidney wanted to show his mother that he had in fact done more with the first twelve years of his life than nothing, and Charlie wanted to show his entire family and all of his friends that he could, when pushed, take and do something seriously.

So when Sensei Duncan told them, after class, that the annual Big Show Sparring Tournament would be taking place in just under two weeks, on Sidney's birthday no less, both boys saw it as more than just an opportunity to put their new skills to use or, as Sensei put it, "To have fun."

Sidney could barely contain his excitement.

This is perfect! he screamed to himself. Mom wants me to make something of myself? How about a karate champion?! She wants to know if I'm more than just a two-bit troublemaker? How about a finely tuned master of the martial arts?!

He had every reason to believe he could win. A fighter by instinct, Sidney could give and take with the biggest and toughest kids the town of Emville had to offer, with one exception, but he would deal with that person later, he hoped.

For Charlie, the tournament came at an equally good time: it was his chance to show his parents, and his sisters, should they dare to attend, and anyone else that he was capable of more than eating an entire bag of double-stuffed Oreos in a single rerun of *Seinfeld*.

"So, who wants in?" said Sensei, holding a pile of registration forms in his hand. "The entry fee is $30. There's a line at the bottom of the page that your parent or a guardian has to sign. You are guaranteed two sparring matches, lunch at the cafeteria and a T-shirt."

Sidney was the first in line.

"I figured you'd want one," said Sensei, handing Sidney a form. "Bring the sheet and your registration fee to class Wednesday night."

There were a few other kids behind Sidney, and then came Charlie. Sensei Duncan did a double take. He did not know what surprised him more: the fact that Charlie was lining up to take part in the tournament, or the look in his eye as he did so.

"Charlie," he said, holding back the form, "this is not a free coupon for chicken McNuggets like I handed out two weeks ago. Are you sure you want one?"

Sensei Duncan had come to understand Charlie over the last few months. He knew what made the kid tick and talk, and although he was surprised to see him in the line, he knew that a gentle bit of teasing would not be a problem.

After a few months as an instructor with the Moran School of Karate, Willie Duncan was getting used to the teaching business and how it worked. He knew how and when to push his students for greater results, and when to back off and let them meet their own goals, if they had any. They were certainly all very different. He had figured that out recently, too. Sidney, for example, was all bluster and energy when he came to class, ready to swing away at any technique shown to him once, and enormously impatient with the intricacies of even the simplest maneuvers. Jeffrey was just the opposite, watching carefully and studying each step with near surgical intensity. Not that Sensei Duncan knew anything about being a surgeon. That was more his brother's line of work. His famous brother, Morris, that is, the all-star wide receiver at Michigan State University who just this past week had decided to accept an offer from Harvard University to pursue his degree in medicine. Morris could talk about the intensity required of a surgeon, and he most certainly would, endlessly, again, the next time the family got together. The mere thought made Willie's skin itch.

He made a note to himself not to think of his brother and the shadow that he cast. Instead, he refocused on Charlie and smiled. This was one of his own students before him, a fellow disciple of karate, and a kid who had come a long way in a relatively short period of time.

"Did you know that?" he said, still teasing. "This is not a coupon for free food. You're going to have to work if you sign one of these sheets."

Charlie's face hardened. "So, you're one of them too?" he said.

Willie frowned. This was not the reply he'd been expecting.

"You're another one who thinks I'm a joke?"

Willie opened his mouth to say something. Nothing came out.

"You think everything's funny for me, don't you? My life's a breeze. Say what you want to Good-time Charlie. You're on their side, aren't you? I knew you were. You look just like them."

Willie peered into Charlie's eyes to see if he could spot anything unusual.

"You probably phone my mom after class and share a laugh about all the lazy things I did."

Sensei floundered for something to say.

"Your dad, too, I bet. My very own school principal. Swapping stories behind my back."

Willie frowned and tried to talk, but he could not, mainly because all of what Charlie was saying was true, except for the part about phoning his mom.

"Well, not anymore, Willie-Boy," said Charlie, holding his hand out. "Just give me the sheet and I'll show you what I mean. And by the way, I don't eat McNuggets anymore. They're deep-fried and full of grease. So are the fries. And their pop is all sugar."

Willie handed Charlie a sheet and watched the boy snap it up and whirl away like an angry secretary. He was struck dumb by Charlie's behavior. He stood and stared with his mouth open and said nothing until all the kids in class had picked up a form.

Then, when the *dojo* was empty, he put on his jacket and turned out the lights. He wondered what form of hell he would have to endure for his comments about those stupid McNuggets.

5.

Charlie's firm resolve to show people what he was really made of softened a bit once he stepped outside.

For one, his legs hurt from all the vigorous kicking and ambitious stretching he had just put himself through. And two, he was hungry.

But Charlie did not give in right away to his desire to plant himself on a bench and chomp on one of the candy bars he had stowed in his backpack. He was truly fed up with the way people viewed him. He knew he brought a fair bit of it on himself, but still . . . enough was enough. It was time to show people what knuckling down and getting the job done was all about.

Besides, what would it look like, putting on the straight face in the *dojo*, then dropping it as soon as he got outside?

It would not look good, he said to himself, so he remained as solemn as he could, which turned out to be a good thing because he was quickly joined by Sidney and Jeffrey.

"So, Charlie," Sidney said as they left the schoolyard behind, "you serious about going in this tournament or what?"

It was just the question Charlie needed to reassert himself.

"You better believe it," he said, feeling stronger just hearing himself talk.

"'Cause it's for real, you know," said Sidney. "It's one-on-one combat, just like the movies."

"I'm ready for it," said Charlie. He had a sudden vision of himself and Sidney squaring off before a gymnasium full of people. Blood slowly oozed from the side of Sidney's mouth as the remains of his last victim settled into his stomach. His eyes glowed green. His mouth opened like the secret entrance to a cave, and he howled like a werewolf as the referee signaled for the fight to begin. Charlie gulped.

"You think Joey's going to be there?" asked Jeffrey.

Charlie's nightmare vision was replaced by the sweet, freckled face of Sidney's ex-girlfriend, the proud owner of the most lethal set of hands and feet in the country. She was the only twelve-year-old who could clean Sidney's clock without breaking a sweat.

"I hope not," said Sidney, clearly unimpressed with the new topic. "She's the only thing between me and the gold. If she's not there, I got it made. If she is, I don't know what I'm gonna do."

Joey did not take karate with the boys anymore. She went later in the evening, with the adults, so she could still have time for her dance lessons.

She had broken off her brief romance with Sidney after he kept asking her to show him how to fight better. "Is that all you want to hang out with me for?" she had said the last time they were together. Sidney had taken too long with his response, so she went back to walking home from school on her own.

"Why do you have to do anything?" said Jeffrey. "Why don't you just meet her in the final and do your best, and if she wins, she wins, and if you win, you win?"

Sidney let out a deep sigh and shook his head. "You know why you never win anything, Jeffrey?"

"I do win things."

"Like what?"

"Math contests. The Chess Challenge. The Lego Master Builder Competition."

"I mean things like karate tournaments," said Sidney.

"I won that roundhouse kick thing Sensei had us do last term."

"I mean things with medals," said Sidney, his impatience growing.

"I got the red ribbon for doing the best *sanchin kata* when that guest instructor was here from Japan."

Sidney could barely restrain himself. "Forget all that. Just answer the question. Do you know why you never win anything?"

"But I'm telling you, I do win things," said Jeffrey.

"He should be asking *you* why you never win anything," said Charlie, chipping in.

"Well, let me just tell you then," said Sidney. "The difference between people who win all the time and people who don't is that the people who win don't settle for just doing their best. They don't even care if they do their best or not. They just want to win. That's what's most important. The winning. So if they win at their best, that's terrific. But if they suck and they still win, then that's still terrific because they still won, and for them, that's what it's all about. Winning."

"So what are you saying?" said Jeffrey.

"I'm saying I'm not going in this tournament to do my best. I'm going in it to win. So when I say I'm not sure what I'm going to do if Joey's there, I mean, I'm not sure how I'm going to get her out of the way so I can win, but I will, because I am going to win this thing. I am going to show my mom that I am not wasting my life."

"That sounds like a pretty tall order," said Jeffrey, using one of his grandpa's favorite statements. "Especially if Joey's there. She's awesome."

"I know she's awesome," said Sidney, starting to worry.

"She's so cool under pressure. That's what makes her so hard to beat," said Jeffrey.

"I don't think it's just that," said Sidney, who was the opposite of cool under pressure.

"I think it is," said Jeffrey. "I think it's exactly that. You can kick like her and strike like her, but she is so cool."

"You know what I think?" said Charlie.

"Should we care what you think?" said Sidney.

"I think your mom should go see a therapist for saying stuff like that to you."

"Charlie," said Jeffrey, as a warning to not say anything more.

"Well, what is she doing, going and telling Sidney that he's wasting his life? That's not something you say to a twelve-year-old kid. You say that to somebody my sister's age, fifteen. Sidney hasn't even had time to waste his life. He just got out of diapers ten years ago. He probably didn't even start sleeping with the light out until five years ago. How's he going to waste his life so fast?"

"My mom already has a therapist," said Sidney.

"Well, tell her she needs another one."

"My mom has one too," said Jeffrey.

"She doesn't need another one," said Sidney. "Nobody has two therapists."

"I don't mean she needs two of them. She needs a different one. Tell her to go to the one Jeffrey's mom has. She doesn't say stupid things like that."

"My mom says stupid things," said Jeffrey.
"She does?"
"You better believe it."
"Like what?"

"I can't think of anything right now. But she does."

"Has she ever said anything like that to you?"

"Probably. Yes."

"I don't mean when she's mad. I mean, has she ever sat you down at the kitchen table like Sidney's mom did and said in a very calm, very rational voice that she thinks you're wasting your life? Has she ever done anything like that before?"

Jeffrey walked in silence for a moment. "She says that about herself enough, but I don't know if I ever get mentioned."

"Well, that's why she's in therapy, right?" said Charlie. "She's got that whole midlife crisis thing going on. My mom talks about this stuff all the time, now that she's over it."

"You don't know that about my mom," said Jeffrey.

"Well, look at her. She's single. She's living with her parents. That's enough to depress anybody, right? We haven't even gotten to her job yet."

"My mom isn't depressed," said Jeffrey.

"Well, maybe not yet. But she's going to be seeing a big number forty on her birthday cake pretty soon, isn't she? And when that happens, look out. If she thinks she's wasting her life now, wait until she sees what the downside of the hill looks like. I heard my mom wore her slippers and a robe for a month after she turned forty. When she turned fifty she was so depressed she could barely get out of bed. She put a box of Kraft Dinner in my lunch one day and told me to tell my teacher to make it."

"My mom is thirty-seven," said Jeffrey. "She still has lots of time."

"My mom's fifty-four," said Charlie. "She has lots of time too, for TV, talking on the phone, yelling at me, telling my sister Crystal to get her butt back in the house."

Sidney did not contribute to the conversation. He thought instead of Joey and how he might get her out of the tournament. He also thought about his mom and whether Charlie was right when he said that she shouldn't be saying those sorts of things.

Sidney didn't know one way or the other how his life was supposed to be going by the time he turned thirteen. He had never done it before, of course. But as his mom was the one person in the world he could count on, and the only person in the world he had ever had to count on, he figured she must be at least partly right. So he went on planning while Charlie and Jeffrey continued to talk.

When they arrived at the corner where they went off in separate directions, Charlie wished everyone a pleasant night's sleep and strode away, happy with himself for not stopping for a bite to eat, and still pleased that he had decided to sign up for the tournament. His stone-faced demeanor was gone, but he was still serious about showing people he could be serious.

Jeffrey walked in silence as he thought about his mom.

Sidney walked in silence and thought about everything he was thinking about.

None of them saw Sensei Duncan combing the streets for Charlie so he could apologize.

6.

Getting the entry form signed for the Big Show presented a bit of a problem for Charlie. First, his mother refused to sign the form, and then his sister Crystal, seeking revenge, came at him with a curling iron.

He encountered his mom first. She was sitting at her command post in the kitchen, at the table with a cup the size of a liter of milk in her hand, sipping hot tea and reading her favorite newspaper, *The National Enquirer*.

"So Britney Spears is really a man," she was saying as Charlie walked in. "I knew there was something phony about her."

Bella Cairns was a big woman with a booming voice and the disposition of a funnel cloud. She was not one to sit back quietly and watch things unfold, and never in her life had anyone found it necessary to prompt her to speak her mind.

Charlie slung his backpack to the floor and sat down on a chair.

"There are cookies in the cupboard," his mother said, without looking up. "I put them there so Banjo wouldn't lick the icing off again."

Banjo was the family dog, and a good friend of Charlie when they weren't getting in trouble together.

"No thanks," said Charlie, gearing up for his request. "I'm in training."

At first Bella didn't respond. She finished the story about Britney, then swigged down another mouthful of tea.

Charlie sat in silence until she said, "You're in what?"

"Training."

"For what?"

"A karate tournament."

She nodded. "Uh-huh."

"I am."

"Sure you are. And I'm running the marathon next week with your father. Now what's the matter? You sick?"

"No."

"Did you eat one of those green hamburgers from the cafeteria again?"

"No."

"You trying to weasel out of phys ed tomorrow?"

"No."

"If that squawk-box Roper was my gym teacher I sure would be."

"I told you, I'm in training for a karate tournament," said Charlie, pulling a piece of paper from his backpack. "Here's the form. You just have to sign it and I'll hand it in." He passed the paper to her, and she read it over.

"Let's see here," she said as her eyes moved down the page. "'The Big Show Sparring Tournament. Competition and fun all rolled into one.' Boy, that Willie Duncan is a clever one, isn't he, making it rhyme like that? He's a real chip off the old block, that one. Just like his old man."

Charlie rolled his eyes and continued to wait.

"It says here there's a thirty dollar registration fee. Who's covering that, Santa Claus?"

Charlie gulped. He had forgotten about the money. "You will, I hope," he said. "I'll pay you back."

His mother read the form again. "Thirty

dollars for a sparring tournament. Wow, they even throw in a T-shirt. That's nice. They make you pay for something you can wipe the blood off your face with. Why don't I just give you a rag you can tuck in your hip pocket? It'll be a lot cheaper, and I won't have to do the laundry. We can just chuck it out at the end of the day."

Charlie stirred slightly in his chair. "There won't be any blood," he said as reassuringly as he could.

"Oh, there won't?" said his mom.

"Not at all."

"So this part down here about 'The Moran School of Karate is not responsible for any injuries incurred during the tournament . . . ,' that's just filling out the rest of the page? They didn't want too much white space on the form?"

Charlie paled. He hadn't realized there was a clause on the registration form dedicated to injuries.

"I think you should take this waste of a tree back to your whatever-you-call-him and say no thanks," said Mrs. Cairns. "Tell that twit that if he wants thirty of my dollars, he's going to have to work a whole lot harder to get them."

Charlie took the form but did not put it away. Instead, he left it on the table and took a minute to collect himself. Then he said, in a voice that he hoped reflected his desire, "I want to show the family that I can take something seriously, and this tournament is the way I'm going to do it." Then he gulped again and resisted an urge to grab a handful of cookies from the cupboard.

Bella downed another shot of tea and put her cup on the table. "Say that again."

"I want to show the family that I can take something seriously, and this tournament is the way I'm going to do it."

She stared at her son. "How old are you?"

"Twelve."

She thought for a moment. "I think your sister Charlotte was fifteen when she fed me a line like that."

Charlie frowned. "What?"

"Susan was nine. She was the earliest. But she took everything seriously anyway. She used to switch off the cartoons so she could listen to the news on the radio. Caitlyn was about fourteen, I think. But she was in love, with Bart or Brad or whatever that little drip's name was. We're still waiting for Crystal. Hopefully she'll come to before she meets a man and has five kids like I did."

"What are you talking about?" said Charlie.

"I'm talking about, big deal, so you want to take life seriously. Go ahead. Take it as serious as you want. But you don't have to spend thirty dollars doing it. Especially when you don't have any money. And especially even more when you can get hurt."

Charlie hesitated. He had not expected this as a reaction from his mother. He honestly believed that he was breaking new ground with his announcement and that the response would be a mixture of shock, respect and admiration. That it would create a buzz in his family that would last at least a week and would get his sister Crystal to forget how mad she was at him.

"You thought you were really gonna rock the boat with this, didn't you?" said his mom. "Well, listen, sonny-boy. I don't read this *Enquirer* nonsense to find out what the freaks in the world are up to. I read it to make sure there are still people out there who are as mixed up as the people in this house are. Now if you want to get knocked silly by a bunch of screaming lunatics, you go right ahead, but not on my nickel. Not when you can just walk into the other room and pick up the newspaper instead of turning on the television. How's that for showing the world how serious you are?"

Charlie licked his lips and thought for a moment. His mother had made several excellent points, particularly the ones relating to blood and injuries, but his head was clear and his stance remained firm: he was entering the tournament.

There was, however, that business about the money that had to be dealt with, and although reading the newspaper would be a far more peaceful way of turning over a new leaf, there was something else to all of this that Charlie wanted to prove.

He glanced briefly at his mom, but she was done talking and back to reading her paper. He thought for another moment, then he sucked up his courage and said, "I'm not talking about taking life seriously. I'm talking about taking this seriously. Karate."

His mother looked up from the paper.

"I want to show you that it's not a joke. That I'm not a joke. That it's something I like doing, and I'm willing to get hurt doing it if that's what it takes to get better at it."

Bella was speechless for a moment. It was true that all of her kids, except Crystal, had come to her at one time or another with a pitch about taking their lives in a new direction. Part of this was because Bella and her husband, Ray, a long-haul truck driver who was rarely home but did his best to stay connected with his family, never pushed their kids to "get serious" or "buckle down" or even to "get going" with their lives. That would happen on its own, Bella believed. The world was too serious all the time anyway. Everyone running this way and that. Parents shopping around for the best schools, the best teachers, the best coaches, the best daycare centers, the best birthing rooms. Is that what living in this place was all about?

Besides, getting serious was the easy part. Anybody could do that. Finding things to laugh about was the challenge, especially when you spent as much time in the hospital as Bella had — as a kid with asthma, when her little sister died of cancer, when her father was killed in the truck crash, when her daughter Susan was born way too early, when her mother had her stroke.

Bella Cairns knew what getting serious was about, and to be honest, she didn't like it.

But at the same time she knew that drive and determination were not exactly bad for a person. She had to admit that although she had shared a laugh or two at Charlie's expense over this karate business, she was truly impressed that he had stuck with it for as long as he had, and a wee bit curious as to why.

"And why don't we let Santa Claus foot the bill?" said Charlie, sensing that the momentum was starting to swing in his favor. "We'll call this an early Christmas present. I'll write you a note so you can pass it on to him as a reminder."

Bella took another sip of her tea. Then she reached across the table and looked at the registration form again. "Let me talk to your father," she said finally. "I'll let you know in the morning."

Charlie had been so excited that he charged right upstairs to his room. He didn't see his sister standing behind his door until she cleared her throat. She showed him the searing hot appliance she held in her hand.

Still smiling, and forgetting for a moment that he was a wanted man, Charlie said, "What are you doing here?"

Crystal smiled back. "I'm here to burn your nose off."

"What's that in your hand?"

"My curling iron," said Crystal. "I'm done with it, and it's still hot, so I thought, since you're coming upstairs in such a hurry, why not use it on you?" She clicked the ends of the curling iron together. "Now, come here. I don't feel like chasing you with this thing." She took a step towards him.

The smile fell from Charlie's face.

"Crystal, wait," he said.

"No."

"You don't know what you're doing."

"Sure I do."

"Stop, Crystal."

"I don't want to."

"Here." Charlie reached desperately into his pocket and pulled out the money he had left over. "Here," he said, showing her the four dollars. "This is for you. This is yours."

Crystal looked at the money. "Where'd that come from?"

"My pocket."

"Where did it come from before that?"

"Um." Charlie did not want her to know that the money had been on him all along. "From Sidney," he said.

"Who's Sidney?"

"My friend. He was with me in the cafeteria."

"That kid with the goofy brush cut?"

"Yes."

"Why did he give you four dollars?"

"He paid me for a magazine."

"Which one?"

"*Vanity Fair*. I was showing him some pictures and he wanted to buy them."

"My *Vanity Fair*?"

"No."

"Then whose?"

"Mine. I bought one for myself."

"You bought a copy of *Vanity Fair*?"

"Yes."

"And you sold it to him for four dollars?"

"Yes."

"Why are you selling him a six dollar magazine for four dollars?"

Charlie gulped. "I owed him two dollars."

"For what?"

"That hamburger I was eating."

"Hamburgers are three dollars."

"I had a dollar in my pocket."

Crystal took the money and continued to stare at her brother. "I'm still going to burn your nose off." She began to move towards him again.

"Please don't," said Charlie, raising his hands to protect himself.

"You said some very mean things to me the other day, Charlie."

"I'm sorry."

"No, you're not."

"It was an accident."

"No, it wasn't."

"It was a mistake. I'm sorry. Honest."

"Not as sorry as you're gonna be."

"I care about you and your bowels. I really do."

"Don't go there again, Charlie."

Charlie felt the wall against his back. "Careful now," he said, trying a new approach. "I can hurt you, you know. You're right in my range for a front kick."

Crystal smiled. "You're telling me to be careful?"

"I'm not the fat, defenseless kid I used to be."

"You look like him to me."

"Watch it," said Charlie.

"Give me your best shot," said Crystal.

Charlie lashed out with a front kick that bumped Crystal's elbow and made her burn herself on the lip. She screeched in horror, dropped the curling iron and lunged at him with the fury of a cyclone. Charlie tried to grab her hands, but they were too fast and furious for him to find, so he gave her a quick shot with his knuckle to the solar plexus, that little spot beneath the rib cage. It stopped her cold.

Crystal bent over and fought to recover her breath. Charlie, breathing heavily from fright, felt around his face for cuts. Then his mother appeared in the doorway of his bedroom.

"What the hell is going on in here?" she said.

Charlie gave her a quick recap.

"You shouldn't tease her about that," said his mom.

"I said I was sorry," said Charlie.

"And you shouldn't attack people like that," she said to Crystal.

"The thing's still hot," said Charlie, picking the curling iron up from the floor.

Crystal stood up straight. A small blister was starting to appear on her upper lip.

"You okay?" said Bella, stepping into the bedroom.

Crystal nodded.

"Go downstairs and get some ice. I'll be down in a minute."

Crystal left the room. Charlie looked at his mom and waited.

"You defended yourself pretty well, I see," she said.

Charlie nodded.

"It's about time."

He kept nodding.

"Is this part of your classes, how to defend yourself against a crazed teenage sister with a hot curling iron in her hand?"

Charlie shook his head. "I just made it up."

His mother looked at him for another moment. "Well, that's good," she said. "I'm tired of saving your behind from her all the time."

"It's the karate," said Charlie, putting in a plug for the tournament.

"I can see that," said his mom.

Then she turned without saying anything more and went downstairs.

The next morning she signed the form and handed him a check for thirty dollars.

Things did not go much more smoothly for Jeffrey.

His mother, Elizabeth, a quiet, reserved woman who worked in a library in the city, was fully aware of the difference karate was making in her son's life and had actually been quite excited when he told her about the tournament. She signed the form straightaway and then asked him about the protective equipment the kids would be wearing. Jeffrey answered her without hesitation: a mouthguard, a cup, gloves and a big helmet like boxers wear in the Olympics.

Elizabeth nodded intently until he stopped talking, then she frowned and said, "That's it?"

Jeffrey, who had thought he was in the clear, frowned back. "What else is there?"

His mother was surprised. "What else is there? Jeffrey, come on. One punch to the nose and you're in the hospital for a week. A kick to the teeth and we're in the hole $5000."

Jeffrey began to worry. His mother's ability to leap to the worst possible outcome of just about any situation was legendary among her friends and family members. "I told you I'm wearing a mouthguard."

"That's not enough, young man," she said, shaking her head. "You're wearing a face mask. I'll borrow one from the McAllisters up the street. Their kids are all into hockey. If you want to play in this tournament, you're going to be protected."

Jeffrey stared at her in silent horror.

"I'm not going to sit here all day worrying about your well-being."

Jeffrey closed his eyes and sagged in his chair. No one ever wore a face mask at karate. It had never been done before. It had never even been talked about before. Not during any of their drills. Not during sparring exercises. Not even when the kids were playing around on their own before class. There were no face masks on the premises. Period.

"Now I know you're probably thinking that I'm being overprotective again, but I disagree."

Jeffrey started to shake his head. "Mom," he said weakly, trying to mount a counterattack.

"Don't 'Mom' me on this one. I'm not moving."

"But you don't understand."

"Oh, yes I do."

"No, you don't."

"Yes, I do. I know how you kids like to look macho with your groovy headbands and your fancy kicks. I see the kids downtown everyday doing it. Mavis Morris and I saw a fight last Tuesday at lunch and one of the boys was kicking just like you. I told Mavis, I said, 'That's what Jeffrey can do,' and she said, 'Watch out.

These kids are out of control with these kicks they're learning.' And she's right. It's not just you. It's everybody."

"But, Mom," said Jeffrey, realizing that he was in a fight for his life. "this is not a street-corner event. There are rules to everything we do. There are going to be referees in every ring, and you can't punch to the head. It's the first thing you learn in sparring. No punches to the head allowed. No punches to the face allowed. It's rule number one."

"Baloney. You get in that ring and it's dog-eat-dog."

"No, it's not."

"Oh, yes it is."

"It isn't anything-eating-anything. It's against the rules to hit in the face."

"Oh, listen to this. It's against the rules to smoke in the library, but people do it."

"Not right in front of you they don't. If you were sitting there watching a guy, he wouldn't light up a smoke because he'd get thrown out."

Elizabeth stared at her son. "Are you tell-ing me that a boy like Sidney Martin is sud-denly going to start following the rules simply because he has to?"

Jeffrey stared right back. "A month ago you were telling me to invite Sidney Martin over to this house for a week to help me take care of Grandpa. You liked him then because he could take care of himself."

"Those were different circumstances," said Elizabeth.

"It's the same kid," said Jeffrey.

"With your grandfather, I trusted him. With you in a ring with a medal on the line, I don't. And I won't. Case closed."

"But, Mom," said Jeffrey, switching to a new approach, "karate is all about tradition and respect. And traditionally, sparring matches did not include face masks. And if you break the rules, you're showing disrespect."

Elizabeth crossed her arms and sat back in her chair. "Traditionally, Jeffrey, they didn't have face masks a hundred years ago, which is why no one wore them."

"But they have them now and no one wears them."

"And don't give me respect for the rules as a reason to not wear one. You should respect what your mother tells you."

Jeffrey fell silent. He had used up all his weapons, or the few he had, at least, and they had gotten him nowhere. Now he was stuck. He took another look at his mom and knew she'd been right all along: she wasn't budging on this one. Not with her arms crossed the way they were. Not with her jaw set the way it was.

He had seen this look so many times in the past, and every time he saw it he knew disappointment would soon be following.

But times were changing in the Stewart household, and Jeffrey was changing right along with them. So instead of caving in and going upstairs to his bedroom and staring at his ceiling all night, wishing with all his might that his mom was a different person, he stuck around and took another crack at her.

"Well, I'm not wearing a face mask to the tournament," he said, crossing his own arms in front of his chest.

"Then you're not going," said his mom.

"Oh, yes I am."

"Oh, no you're not."

"I am not going to look like a geek wearing a face mask at karate."

"I'm not asking you to look like a geek."

"Yes you are."

"I'm asking you to wear a face mask."

"And I'm telling you I'm not."

"Then I'm telling you you're not either. You're not going. No face mask. No karate."

Jeffrey fell back in his chair. Again he felt defeated. His mother was a wall made out of marble, and he was a toothpick trying to break her down. And he had just been feeling sorry for her. Jeffrey recalled the conversation he'd had that night with Charlie and Sidney. Then, from out of nowhere, he started to chuckle. Not a big laugh or anything, just a small, to-himself little chuckle.

"What's so funny?" said his mom.

Jeffrey shook his head. "Nothing."

Elizabeth's frown deepened. "Tell me. What's so funny?"

"Nothing. I was just thinking."

"About what?"

"About nothing."

He started to chuckle a bit harder.

"Don't tell me nothing. What is it about?"

"I can't tell you or I'll get in trouble."

"Is it about me?"

"Yes."

"Then you can tell me what it is."

"No, I can't."

"Jeffrey."

"What?"

"What is so funny?"

"Nothing," said Jeffrey, and his chuckle broke into a laugh. It was all so stupid. But that, of course, was the problem.

"Jeffrey."

"What?"

"Tell me what it is."

"I did tell you."

"No, you didn't."

"I told you it's nothing." Jeffrey looked at his mom and tried to stop himself from laughing, but the look on her face made him laugh even more.

"Jeffrey," said Elizabeth, taking a deep, controlled breath, "this is not going to work out in your favor."

Jeffrey continued to laugh.

"Now I'm willing to bend a bit on this face mask if you can reassure me that you're going to be okay, but not if you're laughing at me like this."

At the mention of the words face mask, Jeffrey's laughter exploded to a new level. If he could, he would tell his mom that he was thinking about when he'd been stuck trying to come up with something stupid she had said to him and of how he now had a perfect example that he would never forget. But he couldn't, so he kept it to himself.

"Jeffrey, I'm ready to scream at you. I'm ready to get really mad about this."

Jeffrey doubled over.

"I'm going to count to three, young man. You have to the number three to tell me what this is about."

Jeffrey could feel the tears running down his cheeks. He wished like crazy that he could tell her, but he knew her reaction would not be a pleasant one, so really, he had no choice.

"One," said Elizabeth.

Jeffrey felt tempted to say something.

"Two."

He pinched his lips shut with his fingers.

"Three."

He shook his head and almost went to the bathroom in his pants.

Elizabeth stared at him for a moment. Through his teary eyes, Jeffrey could see that she was beside herself with fury. Her eyes were smoking slits and her nose and lips were quivering like a bunny rabbit sniffing a carrot, the thought of which made him laugh even harder, since a bunny rabbit was not exactly the animal his mother was trying to imitate.

"Fine," she said, slamming her hand down on the table. "Go to the stupid tournament and wear what you want on your stupid head. But if you get hurt, I'll be the one laughing at you."

She stormed out of the room, and Jeffrey sat there by himself, wiping the tears off his face as his laughter died away, and wondered briefly why she hadn't just said yes in the first place.

Sidney's mom signed his form without saying a word. In fact, she didn't even read over what she was signing. Sidney just pulled it out of his bag and she glanced at it to make sure it wasn't another math test he had failed, signed it, grabbed her coat and told him not to wait up. She didn't give Sidney a chance to tell her about the thirty dollar registration fee or about how important winning the tournament was to him.

On Thursday night the three boys and most of their classmates handed Willie their signed registration forms for the tournament. Willie, relieved that nothing had come of his misguided comments to Charlie, thanked them all and made a point of telling them how proud he was that they had made the commitment to participate. He then singled out Charlie as being especially worthy of praise and said he looked forward to watching him show the others "how it's done."

Charlie was not quite sure how to respond to that comment, and he was too tired to think about it, so he just shrugged and got ready for the class to begin.

And as Sidney waited for Sensei Duncan to stop sucking up to Charlie and start teaching the class, he realized it was time to find out if Joey was going in the tournament or not, and if she was, what he was going to do about it.

7.

Sparring classes were the best, in the opinion of Willie Duncan. There was so much movement and energy, and the competitive spirit in even the most timid of students never failed to rise to the occasion.

There was no better example of this than Jeffery Stewart. Willie remembered the earliest days of Jeffrey's climb to the top of his class. The kid had no idea how to kick or throw a hand strike of any kind, nor did he have the presence of mind to duck during play drills when Willie would sweep a big Styrofoam bat around the class at head level. The idea was to get everyone ducking and jumping out of the way, key skills to have during combat exercises, let alone the real thing. Jeffrey would freeze like a deer in the headlights, and even after

Willie bapped him, he would still stand up-right, as rigid as a fence-post, until his class-mates yelled at him to move.

The problem, as Willie saw it, was that Jeffrey had absolutely no experience with fight-ing of any kind, either real or play, and there-fore was as lost in class as a farmer told to navigate a ship to shore would be, or a lawyer who had to extract a tooth.

But the kid learned quickly. The shell he had lived under for most, if not all, of his life seemed to come off in one piece, for no sooner had Willie told his dad that Jeffrey was a lost cause than Jeffrey began to excel. His front kick snapped like a whip against the heavy bag, and he was the first to understand that the plant foot must turn a full 180 degrees to make the roundhouse kick work. His *sanchin kata* was second to none, followed seemingly over-night by a *konchuan kata* that Willie swore was almost as good as his own. His *kyu kyumite* shone. His *shotu* strikes hurt. His *hojo undo* was the envy of every other student.

And through it all, Jeffrey somehow man-aged to keep his place in the class, which is to say that he never, not once, let any of the praise he received from Willie or any of the several visiting instructors go to his head. He never scoffed at a stupid question or sighed with impatience at the slowness of his classmates. He was always quick to help, and more than once Willie had paired him with a beginner student as a way of speeding up the learning process.

For these reasons, and because, quite simply, no one still took the kid seriously, Willie had unofficially seeded Jeffrey number two in the upcoming tournament. Sidney's ex-girlfriend, Joey, who in a recent adult class had snapped the rib of a police officer who dared her to take her best shot, was number one. Sidney was number three.

In a street fight, Sidney would handle Jeffrey with the enthusiasm of the Cookie Monster demolishing a cookie.

But sparring in an official karate tournament was very unlike street fighting. For one, as Jeffrey and the other kids already knew, strikes of any kind to the head were a no-no. Points were given only when a punch or a kick did not make contact, but surely would have if the attacker had not pulled back. The body, on the other hand, was fair game for anything — kicks and strikes of all kinds — so long as they landed between the shoulders and waist. But Willie knew that Sidney did not appreciate body blows. He was a headhunter. He lived for the glory of a clean shot to the nose or a crisp kick to the ear. Kids like Sidney rarely won the final match because they either continually failed to pull back their assaults, meaning they lost more points than they ever managed to gain, or because while they were looking for a head shot, their opponents were drilling them in the belly.

As with all competitions, there were a few wild cards. Joey's friend Samantha could upset someone if they weren't careful, and a new boy in town, Derek, who had not actually attended a class yet but was allowed to sign up for the tournament after demonstrating to Willie the stuff he had learned at a different school, showed promise. There were also a dozen or so students from a neighboring *dojo* who had been invited to attend. Even the new-look Charlie might win a match if he could stay focused long enough.

Willie loved thinking about who might win the tournament, or who could win if this or that happened. He was the color commentator of his own event that no one else cared about, other than the kids involved and the hundred or so people who would show up to watch.

None of what he thought mattered, of course. First matches were chosen by drawing names from a hat; then the winners went on one side and the losers went to the other, whereupon their names were drawn randomly again. Each participant was guaranteed two fights, but if you lost your second match or any match after your first, you were out.

Each bout had one referee who issued penalties and awarded the points. The first fighter up to three won the match. The referee's word was always final. There were no slow-motion replays or opportunities to challenge a decision. If a point was awarded, it was recorded by the scorekeeper who sat at a table alongside the ring. Fighters who disagreed with a decision ultimately lost their match simply because while they were arguing with the referee, their opponent was battering them with kicks and punches. In other words, the bouts moved along quickly, and if you couldn't keep pace, or chose not to, you would lose.

Willie watched the students in his class perform their various sparring drills. Jeffrey was moving well and seemed at ease with the idea of trying to hit someone, something that had almost made the boy sick the first time he tried it.

Charlie was more attentive than Willie could ever recall, and more flexible, unless Willie's eyes were tricking him.

Sidney seemed preoccupied and stiff, but that was probably just nerves. Willie knew how much pressure Sidney was putting on himself to win, and how that pressure could weigh one down like a sandbag strapped across the shoulders.

He also knew that at any time Sidney could put all of his karate skills together with his natural instincts as a fighter and beat anyone he faced, even Joey.

That was the beauty of tournaments like the Big Show — you never knew for sure what might happen.

8.

Sidney knew what he had to do, but he didn't want to do it in front of his mother. She had never gotten over the fact that her son was dating a girl who could beat him up, so he waited for her to leave. Then he picked up the phone to give Joey a call.

His palms were sweaty and his breath was short, but nothing was going to stop him now, or so he thought.

He dialed the first five digits of her number, then the door burst open and Tizzy returned.

She stared at him for a moment, then she turned and left again.

Seconds later she returned again and slammed the door shut.

Sidney, the phone still in his hand, started to wonder what she was doing.

Tizzy walked towards him and dropped her purse on the table in the dining room.

"Are you done?" she said. She looked as frazzled as Sidney felt, and Sidney knew right away that the phone call he had been about to make had just become number two on his list of problems.

"Done what?" he said.

"Done what?" said Tizzy, her eyes starting to ignite. "What's that thing in your hand, a doughnut? Are you done making your phone call? Are you finished talking to whoever so you can talk to me?"

Sidney gently put the phone back on its cradle. "Yes," he wisely said. "I'm done."

"Good," said Tizzy. "Because I'm done too."

Sidney hesitated. "You're done?"

"That's right."

"Done what?"

"I'm done with this," said Tizzy.

Sidney looked around. "With what?"

"With this," said Tizzy. She took off her coat and flung it in frustration towards the couch in the living room.

"Your coat?" said Sidney.

"No, not my coat. I'm done with this big ball of stress I have in my gut that's been there since I talked with you last week."

Sidney had to think for a moment.

"I haven't slept. I haven't been able to eat. I've been smoking so much Helen brought the fire extinguisher into the coffee room today."

Sidney moved from where the telephone was in the kitchen to the dining room, where he pulled out a chair and sat down. "Who's Helen?" he said.

"You know Helen," said Tizzy, rubbing her forehead.

"No, I don't."

"From work."

"I don't know Helen."

"Helen May or Mayor or whatever her name is. She has brown hair. She's tall. She wears glasses."

"Does she have a tattoo?"

"No. Ruth has a tattoo."

"Is she pregnant?"

"Anita is pregnant."

Sidney frowned. "Oh, is she the one who has that motorcycle?"

"For God's sake," said Tizzy, closing her eyes. "Helen. The woman who drives you home every Friday night when I do cash. She pours you free pop and lets you sit in the lounge to watch the hockey games."

"Oh, her," said Sidney.

"Yes. Her," said Tizzy.

"I thought her name was Ellen."

Tizzy shook her head, which was starting to hurt way more than at any other time during the past few days. "No. It's Helen."

"Are you sure?"

"Of course I'm sure."

"Because I call her Ellen all the time and she always answers."

"Well, her name is Helen," said Tizzy.

Sidney thought about that for a moment. "Why would she answer to Ellen if her name is really Helen?"

Tizzy closed her eyes again, which helped to reduce the pain. "She's being polite. Helen is a very nice person, and she's very shy. She would never think to correct you in case she might embarrass you."

"But if her name is really Helen . . . "

"Sidney," said his mom, "I really don't care about her right now."

"You brought her up."

"I know I did, but I don't care. I'm not sitting here preparing myself to talk to you about Ellen."

"Hey. You just said — ."

"Helen. I meant to say Helen."

"Maybe we should call her to find out what her name is."

"Sidney," said Tizzy.

"Maybe it's you she's being polite to."

"Sidney, enough about Helen. Forget about Helen. She's not what this is about."

Sidney sat back in his chair. "All right. So who is it about then? What are we even doing?" He thought about the important phone call he still had to make and the privacy that was required for him to make it. "Why are you even here? I thought you were going out someplace tonight."

Tizzy took a deep breath and let it out slowly. Then, instinctively, she reached for her purse and dug around for her cigarettes. "I was going out someplace tonight. As a matter of fact, I was on my way to Helen's, which is where I've been going the last several nights to talk about this situation we're in."

"What situation?"

Tizzy struck a match and lit her cigarette. She inhaled deeply, then blew the smoke out as if she were snuffing out a candle. "The situation that started the other day when I told you that you were wasting your life."

A light went on in Sidney's head. Now he knew what she was talking about.

"The situation about our birthdays coming up," Tizzy went on. "That situation."

"What's Helen got to do with it?"

"She's my friend."

"So?"

"So, I've needed a friend lately." Tizzy tried to collect her thoughts. "I feel horrible about what I said to you the other day, Sidney. It wasn't right. It came out wrong. Nothing was good about that conversation we had."

"I could have told you that."

"I was deflecting all the anxiety I was feeling about myself onto you."

"Pardon me?"

"And I'm sorry. For what I said. I am very, very sorry."

"You were deflecting the what?"

"Forget it. It's too confusing."

"How did Helen figure it out?"

"She didn't. I went and saw Dr. Taylor. She set me straight."

"You seemed pretty sure of yourself when you were saying it, you know."

"I know I did. That's what's eating me up

inside. How I must have made you feel." Tizzy shook her head. "I'm sorry. That's all I can say. And that I think you're a great kid and I'm very lucky to have you."

Sidney said nothing. He knew this was very difficult for his mom. She was not a person who said sorry easily.

"I think that with everything we've been through together, the absolute last thing I should be saying to you is that you're wasting your life."

Sidney nodded.

"You're saving my life, that's what you're doing. You're not wasting a life. You're saving one."

Sidney shrugged his shoulders.

"I mean it," said Tizzy, looking him directly in the eye. "You are a very special person."

Sidney looked away and started to fidget in his chair.

"And I have Dr. Taylor to thank for helping me realize that."

Tizzy's eyes started to moisten as she stopped talking. She began to sniff, and before long she was crying as she recalled what she had said to Sidney, and how she had made him feel, and how rotten it had made her feel.

Sidney watched her as she cried and, as

usual when her mood was low, he tried to lift her out of it. "Well, thank goodness for Dr. Taylor then," he said, in an attempt to change the subject.

Tizzy snorted into a Kleenex and nodded her head. "Yes," she said, her voice barely a whisper. "She helped me a lot."

"She usually comes through when you need her, doesn't she?"

"Always," said Tizzy. "Not usually. Always. When I go wrong is when I don't listen to her, and this is a perfect example."

"Huh," said Sidney, to himself but out loud. "And Charlie thought you should switch shrinks with Mrs. Stewart. Shows you what he knows."

Tizzy dabbed at her eyes and blew her nose. The tears had stopped flowing, but she was still upset. "What was that, honey?" she said after a moment.

Sidney hesitated. He hadn't realized he had spoken as loudly as he had.

"Honey?" said Tizzy, waiting for an answer.

"Yes?"

"What was it you just said?"

"Me?"

Tizzy smiled. "There's no one else in the room, sweetheart."

Sidney gulped and licked his lips.

"You said something about your friend Charlie and I should switch something?"

Sidney started to fidget again. "Oh yeah. I did say that."

"What should we switch?"

Sidney tried to throw her off. "Nothing," he said as casually as he could. "I was just thinking about something else."

Tizzy dropped her Kleenex on the floor and pulled out another one from her purse. The crying was starting to make her feel better. "Oh, come on now, sweetie. I've just spilled my guts. You can tell me what's on your mind. I heard you say something about Charlie and I should switch something. Now what was it?"

Sidney did not speak right away.

"Sidney?"

"Yes?"

"Is something wrong?"

"Wrong?"

"Yes."

"No."

"Well, I'd like to know what you think Charlie and I should switch."

Sidney cleared his throat. "Well, one night, when we were walking home from karate,

Charlie said that he thought you should switch shrinks with Jeffrey's mom. But I was just saying to myself that it looks like the shrink you have now is a pretty good one. So what does Charlie know? That's all."

Tizzy stared at Sidney before speaking. "Charlie knows I'm seeing a therapist?"

"I guess he does. Yes," said Sidney.

"Who told him?"

"Um."

"Did you tell him?"

"No. Yes. No. I think he knew. He must have known. I think he just assumed, actually."

"Charlie assumed I was seeing a therapist?"

Sidney shrugged. "He must have."

"Now why would he do that?"

Sidney gulped again. He could see quite clearly that his mother was no longer a blubbering mess but had regained her composure. She was actually looking a little mad at him again.

"Why would he do that?" she said again.

Sidney took in a deep breath. "Well, I told him what you said, and he said that anyone who says things like that should see a shrink, and I told him you already had one, and then Jeffrey said that his mom has one too. Then Charlie said that you should see the same shrink that Jeffrey's mom sees because she never says stupid things the way you do. But then Jeffrey said, 'Sure she does,' but he couldn't come up with any examples. So that's how he knew."

Tizzy said nothing for a moment. Then she sat back in her chair and closed her eyes again and worked at controlling her breathing. Her headache, which had disappeared a few minutes ago, was back with a vengeance.

"Sidney, sweetheart," she said, thinking over each word before saying it, "I don't like it when you tell your friends about private conversations you and I have, okay?"

Sidney nodded his head.

"Honey," said Tizzy, "my eyes are closed. Could you please respond with a word of some kind so I know you're understanding what I'm saying?"

"Okay," said Sidney in a loud voice.

"Okay what?"

"Okay, I understand what you're saying."

"Good." Tizzy paused for a moment. "That goes especially for really stupid conversations we may have."

"Okay."

"And even any bright ones you may feel like bragging about."

"All right."

"I don't want you telling anyone about the things we talk about when we're here at home."

"Okay."

"We agree on that?"

"Yes."

"Good. Thank you, Sidney."

"You're welcome."

Sidney prepared to leave.

"And another thing is," said Tizzy, her eyes still closed, "I really have a problem with you telling your friends that I'm seeing a therapist."

Sidney gulped and sat back down in his seat without speaking.

"Sidney?" said Tizzy.

"Yes."

"Are you there still?"

"Yes."

"Can you see that my eyes are still closed, Sidney?"

"Yes."

"Do you know why they're closed?"

"No."

"They're closed because I have a throbbing headache that keeps returning every time I open them."

"Okay."

"It seems tied to this stress I seem to be having a problem with."

"Okay."

"So for the last time, could you please respond to me with a word of understanding so I know you're hearing me?"

"Okay."

"So did you hear me when I said that I really do not like you telling your friends that I'm seeing a therapist?"

"Yes, I did."

"And you understand that?"

"Yes, I do."

"Do you know why I don't like that?"

"Yes."

"You do?"

"Yes."

"Why?"

"Because only sick people see therapists, and you don't want people to know you're sick."

Tizzy sagged in her chair. Her head tipped back so that, if she did not have a throbbing headache and her eyes were in fact wide open, she would be staring directly at the ceiling.

"Is that the reason?" said Sidney.

Tizzy didn't answer.

"Mom?"

Sidney started to stand up from his chair. "Mom?"

Tizzy brought her cigarette up to her mouth, indicating to Sidney that she had not just suddenly lost consciousness.

Sidney sat back in his chair.

"I'm not sick, Sidney," said Tizzy after an extended period of silence.

"You're not?"

"No."

"Well, that's good."

"I just need someone to talk to once in awhile to help me figure things out."

"Okay. That sounds better."

"Does it?"

"I think so. I think it sounds better."

"It sounds better than saying I'm sick?"

"Yes. A lot better."

"Good," said Tizzy, her eyes still closed and her head still tilted back.

"Can I go now?" said Sidney, taking a chance.

"Yes, you can," said Tizzy quietly.

Sidney sprang up from his chair.

"Thanks for the little talk, by the way," he said, stopping at his mom's side.

"You're welcome."

"I feel a lot better knowing that you don't feel that way about me anymore."

Tizzy managed a thin smile. "Who were you talking to on the telephone?"

Sidney quickly remembered Joey and the tournament.

"Uhh," he said.

"Was it Charlie?"

"Yes," he said. "It was Charlie."

"Don't tell him anything more, okay?"

"Okay."

"You promise?"

"I promise."

"Thank you," said Tizzy.

"You're welcome," said Sidney for the second time, and he carried on to his room.

Tizzy opened her eyes a little and began feeling around in her purse again, this time for her Tylenol.

She did not feel the big ball of stress in her stomach anymore, but she wasn't exactly feeling better about things either, and her head was killing her.

9.

The next week passed quickly.

The boys and their classmates practiced sparring at the *dojo*, working on their combinations and fine-tuning their techniques.

Sidney got hold of Joey and found out that yes, she was going to the tournament, and no, nothing was going to stop her. He was not happy to hear this. It was not in his nature to take defeat lightly, and against Joey, he gave himself almost no chance of donning the Big Show crown. Sidney found himself as stressed going into the tournament as he had been days before when he thought he had to prove himself to his mother.

Charlie was also less than thrilled with the recent developments in his life. True, he had managed to impress his mom beyond her modest expectations of him, and Crystal had not said a word since their altercation in his bedroom. But it was that very altercation that was the source of Charlie's discontent: he felt sick every time he recalled the sensation of nailing her in the gut.

It took him a few days to figure out why he was feeling this way, but when he did, it made perfect sense.

In the past, whenever he and his sister fought, which was often, it was always based on the unspoken assumption that ultimately she would pulverize him because she was older, wiser and tougher, while he was younger, fatter and a bit of a crybaby.

With karate, however, the old assumption no longer applied, and while this was not necessarily a bad thing, especially for Charlie, it was not until after their latest scrap that he realized he now had the potential to actually hurt Crystal if he wanted to. In fact, he could probably break one of her bones if he really set his mind to it, which he could not actually imagine doing, but just having the knowledge that he could was enough to turn him off the martial arts.

In short, the more adept at self-defense

Charlie was becoming, the more frightened of his powers he became. He knew that if the *shotu* he had floored Crystal with — a regular punch, but with the index knuckle on the striking hand extended slightly, changing the nature of the impact from the thud of a small battering ram to the piercing blow of a spear — had struck her in the throat instead of just below her rib cage, she would have been in serious trouble.

The same could be said for his kicks. Charlie was no Jackie Chan when it came to fighting with his feet, but after hours in the *dojo* of kick after kick after kick, even he was starting to get the hang of it, and his legs and feet were toughening up.

Compared to Sidney, and even to Jeffrey, he was still the Pillsbury Doughboy, but put him in front of a fifteen-year-old girl trying to starve herself into a pair of size-two jeans and he was a regular wrecking ball.

Charlie took these concerns of his to his mother on Thursday after school, but their conversation did not turn out very well.

Bella Cairns listened to her son while reading the newest edition of *The Enquirer*. When he finished telling her that he wanted out of karate, and why, which he thought was quite moving, she turned to a page she had already read and showed it to him.

"See this boy here," she said, pointing to a picture that ran alongside the story. "See him? He's a freak. You know why? He has flippers for feet. No toes. They call him Aqua Boy. His parents put him in every circus in the country. They told him if he ever has surgery they will disown him. He's made them rich. The old man quit his job and runs a full-time booking agency. The kid spent two months at Sea World last year and made $50,000. He saw none of it. His mother does all the banking."

Charlie waited for the punch line.

"You know why I'm telling you this?" said his mom.

He shook his head.

"Because you will envy this boy and the life he lives if you drop out of karate right now. You hear me? You will wish you were him if you drop out of karate."

Charlie did not say a word.

His mother closed the newspaper and looked him in the eye. "That first session of classes you were in was free. The rest of them haven't been. Your *gi* was an expense. This tournament is an expense. Your mouthguard was an expense. You want to chuck it all away at a time when you're finally ready to defend yourself? Forget it. Not on my watch. Not when your father's out there driving a million miles a week to put food on the table and have a little bit extra for things like this. You want to take something seriously, go right ahead. But don't come to me saying you're ready and then turn around four days later and tell me you've changed your mind."

Stunned, and thoroughly spooked by the kid in the paper, Charlie retreated to his room, closed the door and sat down to work on his flexibility.

In contrast to his friends, Jeffrey couldn't have been feeling better about the way his week had gone. Classes had been fine. His mom was talking to him again. And while he was quite certain that Joey was untouchable, he did not think that beating Sidney was beyond his reach, and that would likely mean a second place finish in the tournament and a silver medal around his neck.

Not bad for a kid who was afraid of the heavy bag the first time he saw it.

Not bad at all.

10.

Saturday morning finally arrived. In the Martin household, Tizzy awoke first and had her usual sizzling hot shower. She laid a birthday card for Sidney on the kitchen counter and pulled out a package of cinnamon buns that she had hidden in the back of the fridge.

A few minutes later, Sidney stepped out of bed and into his *gi* and emerged from his bedroom ready for combat. He had a birthday card for his mom in his hand, but it was not with the usual flair that he gave it to her. He did not hold it behind his back and make her guess what was on the front of it, or read what he had written out loud so she could thoroughly enjoy every word. He just dropped it in front of her as she sat down at the table with her morning coffee, and then he started doing arm circles to loosen up.

Sidney had gone to bed with his "game face" on. He had spent most of the night staring at the tiny stucco bumps on his ceiling, reviewing his techniques and preparing in his mind for the big event.

He had to be reminded by his mother that it was his birthday too and that there was a card waiting for him on the counter.

"Thanks," he said, opening the envelope.

"How about a birthday hug?" said Tizzy, opening her arms. "It's a day to celebrate, remember?"

Tizzy was in no better frame of mind than Sidney was. She was nervous for him, for one thing, and not at all excited about commemorating the passing of yet another year in her life, for another.

But she was determined to put a happy face on the morning and send her boy off to battle with as much goodness and joy in his spirit as he could handle.

"I have a surprise for you," she said, beginning to beam.

The Martins were not the wealthiest family in town. Tizzy made only a modest income at the restaurant and she steadfastly refused any money from Sidney's father, which was not hard to do, since the guy had never actually offered to give her any. So special occasions like birthdays did not include a heap of presents in the middle of the living room, or an entire day out on the town.

"What is it?" said Sidney.

"Would you like to guess?"

"Not really."

"Not even one?"

"No."

"All right then. Would you like one of your favorite cinnamon buns that I specially ordered myself and even supervised the pouring of the topping to make sure they got enough on?"

"I had one last night," said Sidney.

"You what?"

"I got up in the middle of the night and found them in the back of the fridge."

Tizzy frowned, pulled apart the double bags she had wrapped the buns in and saw with dismay that the package had definitely been opened.

"You had two," she said, taking note that there were only four buns left.

"I was pretty hungry."

"I was going to surprise you with these."

"Sorry."

"I was going to get the candles out and sing Happy Birthday."

"You still can."

Tizzy gave him a look. "Well there's not much point now, is there? You've already eaten half the damn things."

"I didn't eat half."

"Sure you did."

"I had two."

"Well, two-thirds then. Or one-third. Or whatever."

"You didn't say anything."

"I was asleep."

"You didn't say anything before you went to bed."

"Like what? Don't eat the big surprise I have waiting for you in the fridge? You would have been able to go to sleep with that on your mind?"

Sidney shrugged his shoulders. "I didn't sleep anyway."

Tizzy closed her eyes and reminded herself to stay calm. There was no point getting upset over something as silly as a cinnamon bun, especially on Double Birthday Day. So she took in a deep, soothing breath and chose the biggest bun, with the most thick, creamy ooze on top of it, and looked up and smiled at her son.

"All right," she said. "No problem. Would you like another one with me, your birthday twin?"

Sidney rubbed his stomach. "I'm kinda full," he said. "I feel kinda sick, actually."

Tizzy held on to her smile. "That's too bad."

"I think I'm going to go to the bathroom."

Tizzy nodded her head. "That's probably a good idea."

Sidney started to walk past her. "Sorry about that," he said again.

"That's okay," said Tizzy. "We'll try again later."

"Happy Birthday anyway, though," said Sidney, stopping to give her another hug.

"Happy Birthday," she said, taking him into her arms.

They both felt better when they parted.

Sidney's name was drawn first at the *dojo*. His opponent was a boy named Louis from another school. Sidney felt better than he thought he would. He felt calm and focused.

They donned protective gear and stepped into the ring. The referee led them to the center, where they touched gloves, then retreated a few steps to prepare for battle.

His heart stopped beating a hole through his chest, and for the first time in a long time he felt at ease. He was in control. His plan of attack was clear in his head, and as he looked at Louis he saw a kid who was soon to be suffering the sting of a quick defeat.

The referee raised his hand sharply, signaling to the boys that the bout was about to begin. Then, in one quick motion, he dropped his hand like a sword, and Sidney charged. Whap-whap! went his hands. One high to the head, one low to the body. With quick, powerful footwork driving him forward, he scored the first point of the match with a hard shot to Louis's ribs.

Both boys retreated to their sides of the ring. Like goals in hockey, each point in a sparring match is followed by a quick stoppage. Then the referee drops his hand again and the fight resumes.

Sidney charged again and Louis back-pedaled out of the ring. Sidney charged again and Louis tried to fight back with wild punches and kicks that found nothing but dead air.

Sidney scored his second point with a

roundhouse to Louis's shoulder.

Louis came back hard and went after Sidney, but Sidney was waiting for him and calmly put the fight away with a right hand that would have mashed Louis's nose like a soft potato had it not been pulled back.

The final score was 3-0. The match took barely a minute.

The tournament was taking place in the high school gymnasium. There were more than a hundred people on hand to watch, including Tizzy Martin and her friend Helen; Jeffrey's mother, Elizabeth; and Charlie's mom, who brought Crystal along just so she would re-member who she was up against the next time she tangled with Charlie.

The gym was divided into three rings, so while Sidney was snacking on Louis, two other fights were in progress as well.

Jeffrey and Charlie did not do battle in the first round of bouts, but they were both up in the second.

Jeffrey's opponent was a boy named Dennis. Charlie was up against a kid from the *dojo* named Tyler.

Jeffrey won 3-1. Charlie won 3-2.

Elizabeth was shocked as she saw her son spar and move around the small ring. His punches were straight and hard, and his kicks were so fast she could barely follow his feet. Yet it was his confidence that registered the biggest surprise, especially compared to the boy he was fighting. Dennis stood like a frightened bunny before the fight started. His one point came on a combination that seemed more like an accident than a premeditated strike.

Jeffrey had responded with a patient, methodical attack that kept Dennis on the defensive until eventually the boy just became worn out.

When the fight was over, Jeffrey gave his mom a small smile and a quick shrug of the shoulders, as if to imply that the best was still to come.

Charlie was elated with his effort. He had never won anything that required physical effort before. The fact that Tyler was half his size and a full year younger did not dampen his spirits. Even if his joy had dipped a bit, Bella would have jacked it up with another pep talk.

She had given him one at the breakfast table earlier in the morning.

"Now look," she had said, smearing a swath of peanut butter across her toast, "about yesterday, and that discussion we had about the kid with the funny feet. I don't want you to get the wrong idea. I appreciate the fact that you're not a violent person. I like that about you. But what you're learning over there at that hojo or whatever you call it, that's not about being mean to people. That's about protecting yourself. That's about protecting your sisters if they ever need it. And protecting me, for that matter, touch wood it never happens. So don't you go feeling bad about learning this stuff. And when you get into that ring today, don't you hold back anything. These are all kids who are used to it. Besides, you'll have so much padding on, you won't even know you've been hit."

It had worked.

"How'd I look?" said Charlie after the fight, his face shining with sweat.

"Like a big kid swatting around a small kid. But don't worry about that. You did fine."

Crystal had been a bit harsher. "That kid practically had to sit on your lap to reach you."

"He was pretty quick," said Charlie, getting ready to return to the action.

"He was scared of being trampled to death," said Crystal.

Sidney and Jeffrey fought again in round three.

Again, both of them won.

The tournament was unfolding just as each boy thought it would. But at the same time the field of fighters was starting to get smaller in number, and since there was no room at the top for all three of them, one of the boys would be losing very soon.

11.

To no one's surprise, Charlie was the first to go out. But what did startle people was the way in which he lost: his nose was bleeding and his lip was cut, but he refused to leave the ring until his opponent scored his third point, which took a lot longer than anyone thought it would.

The fight was bad for Charlie right from the start.

For one thing, the kid he was fighting, Bradley, was the exact opposite of tiny Tyler. Bradley had arms like tree branches, and what he lacked in speed he made up for with unbridled aggression. He snorted at Charlie when the two touched gloves to begin the match, and each time he threw a punch his eyes lit up like the fiery end of a rocket on a launchpad.

His kicks were as lumbering as a crane hoisting a steel beam, but when they connected, they rocked Charlie like a missile thudding into a mountain.

Bradley went up 1-0 early with a shot to Charlie's ribs. Charlie gamely fought back and evened the score when he countered one of Bradley's thunderous jabs with a neat side kick that connected just enough to register.

From there, however, the bout got ugly.

Bella and Crystal, sensing that their boy was in over his head, started hollering for better refereeing, which got Bradley's supporters calling for a higher class of opponent.

Then, during a brief spurt of infighting, where both Charlie and Bradley connected with a series of frenzied punches and strikes, but neither landed anything worthy of an actual point, Bradley unloaded a clean shot that caught Charlie, who was trying to duck, flush in the face. Blood spurted from Charlie's lip and immediately began flowing from his nose. The ref called for time and with a moist cloth mopped up Charlie's mug to see what the damage was. Bella Cairns rushed over to join the inspection, as did Willie Duncan, who was also watching the fight.

"It's over," said the referee.

"You better believe it's over," said Bella.

"Sit down and take it easy, Charlie," said Sensei Duncan.

"Forget it," said Charlie, stepping aside. "It's up to three and he's only got one. Actually, he just lost one. I'm winning." He wiped his nose and looked at the blood on his glove. For a moment he felt squeamish enough to faint, but he stood tall, wiped his glove on his pants and motioned Bradley to continue.

"The fight is stopped," said the referee.

"No, it's not," said Charlie. "I got something to prove here. Now, let's go."

Bella ended her intervention. She saw the determination in her son's eyes. She saw the blood he had wiped from his nose. She looked at the ref and thought for a moment, then motioned for him to resume the match.

Crystal couldn't believe it. "Mom, what are you doing? He's gonna bleed to death. That guy's gonna kill him."

"Oh, pipe down," said Bella, feeling something towards her son she had never experienced before. "Let him go on."

The battle went back and forth. Charlie scored once, but Bradley notched two points of his own with haymakers that could have leveled a medium-sized horse.

Finally, wheezing for breath and sick from the taste of swallowing his own blood, Charlie's guard, for what it was worth, began to drop. Bradley moved in for the kill and got it with a front kick right up the middle of Charlie's belly.

Charlie received a standing ovation from the crowd that had gathered to watch. Crystal handed him her bottle of water and dabbed at his nose with a T-shirt she had snatched from someone else's gym bag.

Sidney ran over to pat him on the back. Jeffrey whispered in his ear that he was amazing. Joey came over to give her old friend a hug. And when he sat down on a bench to recuperate, his mom came up beside him and ran her fingers through his hair.

"All right," she said. "You did it."

Charlie nodded. He had done it. He had proven it to himself more than anyone else, and that, he knew, was the most important person of all.

"Enough already," said his mom. "You're not pretty enough to do this more than once."

Charlie nodded again and settled in to watch the rest of the tournament and cheer on Sidney and Jeffrey.

12.

Sidney had taken in Charlie's match with a mixture of admiration and bewilderment.

Sure, Charlie had shown the world how courageous and serious he could be, and that business about waving off the ref with blood all over his face was double thumbs-up all the way, but what kind of strategy was that for such a big fight?

Sidney knew that to beat a hammer-thrower like Bradley you had to get low, make him place his shots and think a little, and attack him from every angle with every punch and kick in the book.

Charlie had just stood there, like he was hoping Bradley would flat-out miss the target with his punches, which he did, but not often enough to lose the bout.

Sidney could see himself toying with Bradley like a kid teasing a kitten with a ball of wool. He would move around a little, bob and weave a little and let the big lug have it whenever he stepped into range.

It would be no contest. Three to nothing for sure.

So Sidney silently stroked Bradley off the list he was carrying in his head of people he had to be concerned about and turned his attention to his pal Jeffrey.

Jeffrey was fighting a kid named Owen, who Sidney had never seen before. In another match, Joey was going against Derek, the boy who had auditioned for Sensei last week. Sidney couldn't bear to watch Joey do battle — it was too demoralizing — so he pretended she wasn't there.

Jeffrey looked good in his fight. He moved smoothly around the ring and he wasted no energy on maneuvers that stood little chance of reaching their target. Owen apparently believed Jeffrey was incapable of doing much, for he charged in shortly after the fight started and found himself quickly down by one from a kick that came within an inch of his head.

Regrouping, Owen moved in again after

the break, this time in a crouch, as if he sensed that Jeffrey was unskilled as a marksman. Proving him wrong, Jeffrey tagged him at least once with a stiff right hand and would have banged him again had the ref not pulled him away.

Up 2-0, Jeffrey played it smart and let Owen come right to him again. When the kid was in range, and so desperate to get a point that he forgot all about defense, Jeffrey let him have it with a roundhouse high to the ear. Again, it was pulled back in time, and Owen was over and out.

Since the fight had been brief, Sidney had little choice but to watch Joey. He was stunned by what he saw. Down 2-0 on penalty points, she fought back to tie the score at two, but was again dinged for a punch that, according to Derek's reaction, caught the boy flush on the nose.

Frustrated by all the penalties she was getting, Joey lost her cool and took issue with the referee. Derek saw his opportunity and went for it. He caught her with a quick kick to the chest and Joey, her face a combination of fury and shock, was out. She'd lost her match to a no name, and Sidney could no longer sit still on the bench.

He leapt to his feet but caught himself before he could celebrate. Joey was a mess, and she was furious.

"He cheated!" she cried at the referee. "He cheated! Every time I threw something at his head, he'd make it look like I hit him. I never hit him. He'd be dead by now if I hit him. He'd be running around looking for his head."

Sidney looked at Derek. He was a tall boy with long, dark hair and big hands and feet. He had a towel up to his face, as if to soothe a sore spot, but as he walked away, Sidney swore he saw the towel come off for an instant and the flash of a smile.

He turned back to Joey. The ref had not listened to her plea, but she was not crying anymore. Her breathing was still heavy and her face was as red and ferocious as Sidney could ever recall seeing it, but the tears had stopped.

Joey was not one who cried often, or for very long.

"You got robbed," said Sidney, who still could not believe what had happened.

"If I ever see that kid outside this stupid gym . . . " said Joey through clenched teeth, throwing her towel into her bag. "He's a cheater. He's a little wimp cheater."

Although Joey was angry and frustrated,

she was also speaking the truth and giving Sidney, who would be fighting Derek next, fair warning. The kid was a cheater, and if Sidney wasn't ready for him, he'd be sitting beside Joey when the final came around instead of going for the crown that he was suddenly so sure was his.

13.

Tizzy Martin sat in the bleachers and watched her son. She knew he was absolutely dying to win the Big Show. She knew how competitive he was. She knew he was one fight away from reaching the final. Still, she was a bit surprised to see him pacing along the far wall of the gym, going over again and again in his head all the things he had to do to win his last two fights. He ignored anyone near him. He moved as if he was in a trance. Tizzy didn't get into sports so she wasn't really sure what he was doing. But her friend Helen apparently followed every sport in the book.

"See," Helen said at one point, just as Tizzy was about to worry. "He's visualizing his opponent right now. He's in the ring with him.

He's throwing punches. See? Look. He's moving his hands like he's about to throw a punch."

Tizzy nodded. To her, Sidney looked like the guy with the funny hat and big overcoat who hung around outside the restaurant some afternoons, muttering to himself until someone came and picked him up and took him back where he came from.

"He's very intense, isn't he?" Helen was saying as Tizzy popped out of her own thought bubble.

"Yes, he is," she said. She could feel the ball of stress returning. Was it healthy for a boy of such a young age to be so caught up in an event that he actually paced around and talked to himself in front of a hundred other people? Or did all this still have something to do with that comment she had made to him about wasting his life? She honestly did not think so. Tizzy felt she had dealt with that effectively enough. But how do you know with a boy who keeps everything inside all the time? Plus it was his damn birthday on top of everything else. Hers too, of course. Could there be a way of putting more pressure on the kid? Was there possibly a little girl in a hospital bed somewhere who wanted to reach out and tell

Sidney that if he won the tournament, she would get better and walk again?

Good grief, Tizzy thought to herself. The pressure was getting to her too, now, as the final fight of the day drew near. Joey losing didn't help. With her still in the picture, Sidney had seemed almost content with the idea of placing second, but now that she was out, Tizzy could tell his insides were churning ten times faster than they had been.

Having Helen with her wasn't turning out to be such a grand idea either.

"Some people say sports is 99 percent mental and 1 percent physical," Helen was saying.

"Well," Tizzy said, somewhat absently, since a discussion on sports was not what she wanted at the moment. "It must be more than 1 percent, don't you think?" She kept her eyes on Sidney as she spoke.

"That's what I read in a magazine," said Helen, who often quoted from magazines. "I think it was a story on Tiger Woods. You know he was four years old when he drove his first golf ball off a tee? Four years old. And you know, he two-putted the first green he was ever on. His ball landed on the green, and he two-putted it to the hole. That is so amazing."

Tizzy took in a deep breath and stayed quiet. She had never watched a game of golf in her life and knew the name Tiger Woods only because he was absolutely everywhere.

"I mean, you know, when you think about it, he wouldn't have even known how to line up a putt. He must have just stood over the ball and whacked at it and it went in. That is so amazing."

Tizzy looked down at the gym floor. In the one remaining ring she saw Jeffrey taking on that big Bradley thing who had chewed up Charlie. The winner of this fight would take on the winner of the bout between Sidney and Derek for the championship.

Tizzy was impressed with Jeffrey. His mom was a bit of a mouse, sitting way over on the other side of the gym by herself, but Jeffrey was a kid who had a lot more guts than she had ever imagined.

"And you know, today, he gets on the green, it's like money in the bank," Helen went on, still talking about Tiger. "His record heading into the final round of play, when he's in first or second place, is something like twenty-five wins and one loss. Or something like that. I can't remember for sure. But it's something amazing like that."

Tizzy nodded.

"Because, I mean, you know, he is playing against the best golfers in the entire world. Not just in America, but the entire world."

Tizzy looked down at Sidney again, but he was not pacing around where he had been before. He had returned to the land of the living and was now watching Jeffrey fight. Tizzy could tell her son was nervous. Jeffrey seemed to be in the groove of his life at the moment, dancing away from Bradley's missiles and nipping in for quick punches and kicks that were either landing or just barely missing. He was such a wisp of a kid, Tizzy almost felt sorry for Bradley having to try to find him in the ring, much less contain him long enough to get a piece of him.

"There's South Africans," she heard Helen say beside her. "Spaniards. Irish. British."

Bradley scored a point to tie the match at 2-2. Tizzy glanced at Sidney and could tell he was pulling for Bradley to win. He was a much bigger, slower target for Sidney to connect with. Jeffrey, on the other hand, was like trying to catch smoke.

"And in that article, they talked about sports being 1 percent physical and 99 percent mental."

Bradley looked like he scored the winning point on a kick, but apparently Jeffrey blocked it with his forearm.

Sidney stood as stiff as a board and watched alongside the ring.

"So it's not just me making it up," Helen said. "It's an actual piece of journalism."

Tizzy was transfixed by the fight below. Both boys were putting up a tremendous effort. Come on, Bradley, she said to herself. Pop him one. Catch him. Get him!

"So I don't know if you can just question it or not," said Helen.

A moment later, the match was over. Tizzy didn't see the final point occur, but one quick look at Sidney told her it was a legitimate one. A longer look at Jeffrey drove it home. The kid was beside himself with emotion.

"I don't know what you think," said Helen, who was completely unaffected by the outcome of the match.

Tizzy was drained. "I think I need a cigarette," she said.

Helen gave her a look. "What does that have to do with anything I've just been talking about?"

"Nothing," said Tizzy, rising to step outside.

She was now in a bit of a trance of her own. Her son looked like he was ready to barf, and the big thug, Bradley, who she was relying on to beat Jeffrey, had just lost.

"Well, you know, that was a whole magazine article I shared with you," said Helen, picking up her purse.

Tizzy ignored her and started to head for the doors.

"And Tiger Woods can teach us all a lot about winning and losing."

Tizzy shook her head and wondered for a moment how much it would cost to rent that sparring ring so she could show Helen what she truly thought of her and her magazines.

14.

Sidney knew he was in trouble against Derek before the fight began.

It had nothing to do with Derek himself. Sidney could crunch him like a nacho chip if they ever met in the schoolyard.

But Sidney was having a hard time concentrating. He was giving himself a headache from clamping his teeth too hard on his mouthguard, and every time he tried to focus on Derek, his mind would race away to something else. He was agitated. He was antsy and jittery. He couldn't stop moving, even when he was told to stand still, and everyone, from his mom wishing him good luck to the referee going over the rules one more time, was ticking him off. Come on, he felt like telling them, get outta the way and let me smoke this kid.

In other words, Sidney was not cool for this fight. He was not calm and clear-headed. He was a mess and he knew it, and every time he tried to do something about it he failed, which made him even more frustrated than he had been.

To make it worse, Derek was a sneaky fighter. Against Joey, every time she had sent a kick at his head, he had made it look as if she had hit him. Once he even toppled over and pretended to be hurt.

He did the same thing against Sidney, and again it worked to perfection.

Down 1-0 early in the fight, Sidney was given a penalty point for kicking Derek below the belt, which he had not done, but Derek went down as if he'd been hoofed by a mule, and the referee bought it.

Derek scored his second point after catching Sidney with a double front kick combination that came after a second warning to Sidney from the ref to keep his kicks away from Derek's head. So incensed had Sidney been that he practically spit his mouthguard out to protest, which was when Derek made his move.

Sidney fought gamely on after that, but being down by three was a hard place to win from, and all cheating and trickery aside, Derek was actually a more skilled opponent than Sidney had given him credit for.

The final score was 3-1. Without question, it was Sidney's worst fight of the tournament. He lost three points for illegal contact.

Tizzy burst into tears when the final point was awarded. Sidney stood stock-still and tipped his head back and closed his eyes. This was a moment of truth for him. The old Sidney would have been rampaging around the ring by now, but something quite incredible was about to happen.

Calming himself with a pair of deep breaths, Sidney reached out and shook Derek's hand. Then he removed his sparring gear and ran over to where Jeffrey was standing.

The final match of the day would take place in thirty minutes, and Sidney wanted to make sure Jeffrey knew everything he needed to beat Derek and win the Big Show.

So Sidney became Jeffrey's unofficial coach and top cheerleader.

Up in the stands, Tizzy could not figure out what was going on. She had expected her son to be paralyzed with disappointment or raging with frustration or at least bummed at not even finishing second.

Instead she saw him helping Jeffrey in every way he could. Charlie joined in and so did Joey, but it was Sidney who led the way. He came up with the idea that Jeffrey should rock Derek with a real kick to the head as soon as the match started, and he also pumped Jeffrey so full of confidence that Jeffrey went out and did just that.

Early in the match, he launched a round-house that caught Derek flush on the cheek. The kid went down as if he'd been hit by a bullet. The ref warned Jeffrey that one more strike like that and he was disqualified. He also told Jeffrey that, as far as scorekeeping went, he was at -1.

Jeffrey nodded and waited for Derek to stand up, which took awhile.

When the fight resumed, he sent another kick towards Derek's head, and instead of stand-ing in to make it look like a connection had been made, Derek leapt out of the way to avoid getting hurt again. Jeffrey went after him. Sidney's tactic had worked: Derek was no longer thinking like an actor; he was trying to survive.

Jeffrey scored his first point with a front kick to Derek's chest. His second point came on the combination Sensei Duncan had shown them all in class, but that Sidney made come alive in the hallway outside the gym.

"You have to wait a split second for him to respond to the first punch before you throw the second one," he had said. "Otherwise you're not giving him any time to move his hands. You're throwing the big fake to his head, but if you don't give him time to get his hands up, you're just going to throw a punch to his gut and he'll be right there to block it. You have to give him a second to respond."

The next two points came on identical roundhouse kicks that Derek had wanted no part of. He was not quick enough to move out of the way, and Jeffrey knew exactly when to pull back to avoid an actual hit.

Just two minutes into the final bout, Jeffrey was crowned the new Big Show champion.

Charlie and Sensei Duncan hoisted him onto their shoulders. Joey embraced Sidney for a coaching job well done. Jeffrey's mother, Elizabeth, sat up in the stands and stared as if she was watching someone else's child. Across the gym floor, Tizzy did the exact same thing.

15.

The celebration that followed the tournament took place at Kelly's Roadside Attraction, where Tizzy and Helen worked.

The staff presented Tizzy and Sidney with matching birthday cakes.

Bella bought Charlie a banana split, which took him longer to eat than any other serving of ice cream he'd ever been given in his life.

"I'm not kidding," said Bella. "When he was sixteen months old we gave him a bowl of vanilla ice cream and he gobbled it up so fast he frightened us. My husband turned to me and said, 'Don't you feed this child?' I said, 'Yes, but I've never seen anything like that before.'"

"It's because of my mouth," said Charlie, whose lip was thoroughly swollen.

"I know why it is," said his mom. "I just still can't believe it."

Jeffrey was given his pick of the menu. He chose lasagna and shared it with his mom. He knew she hadn't eaten anything all day.

Everyone congratulated Jeffrey for his incredible outing, but it was Charlie's grim-looking face and Sidney's conversion from warrior to teacher that got all the attention.

For Charlie, it was all quite simple to explain.

"We all got what we wanted," he said. "A chance to show a different side of ourselves."

Sidney nodded. He had not been aware that offering to help Jeffrey would be seen as such a big deal. Really, all he was doing was trying to make sure that that big stick Derek didn't win anything. He wasn't trying to show people that he was a great sportsman or a good loser or that, in the span of twenty seconds, he had put everything the tournament was about into perspective and come up with friends helping each other out as the ultimate reward for participating, with winning being a distant second prize.

But he could see how people would interpret his actions that way. He figured he would surprise a few people by not throwing any chairs or going after Derek at the conclusion of the fight.

The truth is, though, he had thought about doing just that, throwing a chair and going after Derek, but when he closed his eyes and took those deep breaths, he suddenly saw himself not as a loser in a ring, but as a kid who still had something to offer, even though things hadn't gone the way he'd wanted them to.

So was that such a big thought to have? Did that make him wiser or more valuable to society than he was before?

"No," said Tizzy when he asked her after they got home. "But you just became a lot bigger as a person for what you did today. So did Charlie. So did Jeffrey. People can't talk about you in just one way anymore."

Sidney smiled when he heard that.

Tizzy lit another cigarette and leaned back in the couch. "Of course, they will anyway. That's how people are. But you'll know, and I'll know, and that's good enough."

Sidney closed his eyes and thought for a moment and decided that maybe he was ready for thirteen after all.